George Washington

Father of Our Country

George Washington
Father of Our Country

A FIRST BIOGRAPHY

BY

David A. Adler

ILLUSTRATED BY

Jacqueline Garrick

Holiday House/New York

IMPORTANT DATES

1732	Born, February 22, in Westmoreland County, Virginia.
1743	Augustine Washington, George's father, dies.
1749	Is appointed surveyor of Culpeper County, Virginia.
1753	Becomes a major in the Virginia army, and later a lieutenant colonel.
1755	Serves with General Braddock in the French and Indian War.
1755–1758	Becomes commander of the Virginia militia.
1759	Marries Martha Custis, January 6.
1758–1775	Becomes a member of the Virginia House of Burgesses.
1775–1783	Becomes commander in chief of the Continental army.
1781	Defeats Lord Cornwallis at Yorktown, Virginia.
1787	Is elected president of the Constitutional Convention.
1789	Is elected first president of the United States and inaugurated on April 30.
1792	Is reelected president of the United States for a second term.
1796	Publishes his farewell address.
1799	Dies at Mount Vernon, December 14.

CONTENTS

1. *Young George*

George Washington was born on the morning of February 22, 1732 in a simple four-room farmhouse in Westmoreland County, Virginia. In 1732 Virginia was settled mostly along the waterways. But even much of what was called settled land was either muddy swampland or overgrown with trees. Here and there were some tobacco fields and smaller fields of wheat and corn.

There were some wealthy plantation owners in Virginia who lived in a grand style with beautiful furniture, silks, china and silverware. They had many slaves, but most Virginia farmers lived more simply.

George Washington's father, Augustine, was not a wealthy plantation owner. The Washingtons owned many silver spoons, but all their forks were whittled from wood. They had thirteen beds in their house but not enough good sets of sheets to cover them all. Augustine Washington owned several thousand acres of land. He also owned some slaves, but not enough to work all his land. Most of his land remained un-cleared.

Augustine Washington

Augustine Washington was tall and broadly built. He was strong, gentle and ambitious. A few years before George was born, iron ore was discovered on Augustine's land. He became a partner with an English company to mine the ore and built an iron furnace. In 1729 he sailed to England to meet with his partners. He returned home, almost a year later, and was shocked to learn that his wife, Jane Butler Washington, had died while he was gone. Augustine was left with a household to manage and three children, Lawrence, Augustine Jr. and Jane.

In March 1731 Augustine married his neighbor, Mary Ball. She was twenty-three years old, had light blue eyes, blond hair and rosy cheeks. Eleven months after Mary Ball married Augustine, their son, George, was born. Within the next several years she gave birth to Betty, Samuel, John Augustine, Charles and Mildred.

Mary Ball Washington was a hard, bossy woman. She seemed to be always worried, always afraid. When young George went outside to play, she insisted that he stay close to the house. When he was older and went to school, she didn't let him go alone.

In school George learned to read but he never was a lover of books and great literature. Much later, when he had books of his own, many were practical. They explained things like how to care for horses, how to run a farm and how to build things from wood.

George learned to write in school and had good handwriting. He often practiced his writing by copying maxims, rules of proper behavior. Among the rules he copied were, "Kill no vermin, fleas, lice, or ticks in the sight of others," "Cleanse not your teeth with the tablecloth," and "Keep your fingers clean."

George had difficulty with spelling. He wrote *blew* when he meant blue and *oyl* when he meant oil. But arithmetic and numbers interested him. He liked to multiply, divide and measure things. While other children might ask "Why?", young George wanted to know "How many?"

After George's half brothers Lawrence and Augustine Jr. had learned to read, write and do arithmetic in Virginia, George's father sent them to schools in England. But George's father died in 1743, when George was just eleven. And George's mother had no intention of sending him anywhere to study. She needed George to help manage the Washington household.

Mount Vernon

2. *The Young Surveyor*

The Washingtons lived in a house they called Ferry Farm. It was on the bank of the Rappahannock River. When Augustine died, George inherited Ferry Farm, some land and ten slaves. The will directed his mother to manage the house, land and slaves until George was old enough to do it himself. She kept George's property for many years. Some claim she never gave it up, that George did not get his inheritance until his mother died forty-six years later.

George's mother also had property of her own. But she still complained. Years later, when George was the general of the colonial army, she complained that she had to borrow corn in order to survive. She complained that she was so poor, she might starve. But this wasn't true. George cared well for her.

Young George left Ferry Farm whenever he could. Often he went to Mount Vernon, the nearby home of his half brother Lawrence. He was an outspoken man with an easy smile, and George admired him.

Ferry Farm

Lawrence had married Anne "Nancy" Fairfax, the daughter of William Fairfax, a rich and influential man. And her cousin, Lord Thomas Fairfax, was the largest landowner in Virginia, with more than five million acres. Lawrence, Nancy and her family introduced young George Washington to the life-style of the small number of Virginia people with the time and money to dress in the latest fashions, play cards and go fox hunting.

When George wasn't busy with Lawrence and Nancy's elegant friends, he enjoyed surveying, the measuring and mapping out of land. With instruments which had belonged to his father, George practiced surveying a turnip field, a small pine forest and other small patches of land.

In 1748 George looked older than his sixteen years. He was more than six feet tall. He had reddish-brown hair, blue-gray eyes, a large straight nose and huge hands and feet. Nancy's cousin, Lord Fairfax, gave this old-looking young man a job. He sent George on a month-long expedition to help survey some of his land.

At one time during the expedition, George wrote in his diary that he was given a threadbare blanket with "double its weight of vermin such as lice and fleas." He was glad to get up the next morning and give back the blanket. And George met some Indians who, he wrote, "were coming home from war with only one scalp." George watched them do a war dance. He was learning firsthand about the American frontier.

George went on other surveying expeditions. At seventeen he was appointed official surveyor of Culpeper County. He used much of the money he earned to buy land of his own.

When George wasn't working, he enjoyed playing cards and billiards. And he began to have an interest in women.

Young George did not have an easy time with them. Once, while he was swimming naked in the Rappahannock River, two young women stole all his clothes. And at parties, George was often too nervous to speak. When he did speak, he wasn't himself. He was boastful.

George was quickly becoming a responsible adult. In 1751 his brother Lawrence became ill with tuberculosis. George went with Lawrence on the long boat journey to Barbados in the West Indies. They hoped the warmer climate would be good for Lawrence.

George took care of his brother until he himself got sick with smallpox. George recovered in three weeks. But the disease left his face, especially his nose, scarred with pockmarks.

George went home. He planned to return to Barbados with Nancy, his brother's wife. But before they could leave, Lawrence arrived in Virginia, no better than before. He died a few weeks later in Mount Vernon.

Lawrence had been an officer in Virginia's volunteer army. George applied to replace him. In 1753 George was made a major and charged with training others in southern Virginia to fight. At twenty-one, George was a soldier and a leader of men.

3. Commander of Virginia's Army

Soon after George was made a major in the Virginia army, he was sent on a long and dangerous mission. He traveled on horseback to the Ohio River Valley to warn the French to get their troops off British land. Six men traveled with Major George Washington—a guide, an interpreter and four servants. After many weeks, they met the French military commander. He told George that the French would not move.

It was winter when George began the long trip back to Virginia. It was bitter cold, and snow covered the ground. Along the way an Indian shot at George at close range and somehow missed. George fell off a raft into an icy river and almost drowned. Finally George let most of the men stay behind and wait with the horses for warmer weather. He walked ahead with the guide and brought the message from the French commander to the British governor of Virginia.

George was promoted to the rank of lieutenant colonel. He was told to gather an army, travel back to the Ohio River Valley and defend British rights.

George gathered 160 men, and a few months later was on his way to fight the French. George and his men found a small force of French soldiers. They surrounded the soldiers and attacked. Washington's forces easily won the battle. This was the beginning of what was known in America as the French and Indian War. It would last nine years, from 1754 until 1763.

After their first battle, George and his men built a fort, Fort Necessity. It was built in a poor location on low land near a creek. It was easy to see inside the fort from the higher land nearby. When it rained water flooded into the fort, turning it into a sea of mud.

The French attacked Fort Necessity in a heavy rain. George's men could hardly fight back. They were hungry, and their gunpowder was wet. After nine hours they surrendered. Nevertheless, when Washington and his men returned to Virginia, they were praised for their bravery.

Soon after that, the British lowered the rank of all colonial officers. George refused to lose rank. He resigned instead and returned to Virginia farm life.

George rented Mount Vernon from Lawrence's widow. Later, when she died, he inherited the estate. This time his stay at Mount Vernon wasn't long. Within a year he was back in uniform as an aide to British General Edward Braddock.

George Washington accompanies
General Braddock in his coach

Braddock was on a march with more than one thousand soldiers. They wore the bright red uniforms of the British army. They were going to the Ohio Valley to fight the French. Following close behind them were wagons loaded with supplies and cannons.

The British soldiers were easy targets for the French and Indians hiding in the surrounding forest. The Indians made shrill war cries. Then, along with the French, they shot at the British. The British panicked. Washington wanted to lead the men to relative safety behind rocks and trees, but Braddock refused to let him. Braddock ordered his men to fight in the open like brave British soldiers.

Two of the horses on which George Washington was riding were shot. His hat and uniform were hit several times. He wasn't harmed, but hundreds of other British soldiers were killed, including General Braddock.

George Washington rode back to Mount Vernon. He felt discouraged, but still he loved the military. He loved the sounds and danger of battle. When Governor Dinwiddie asked George to become the commander of Virginia's army, George accepted. That was in 1755. Commander George Washington was just twenty-three years old.

Three years later, in 1758, Commander George Washington, along with colonial and British soldiers, set out to attack a French fort. By the time they got there, the French had already left the Ohio Valley and moved north. A year later the French surrendered. The British were in control of the colonies, the frontier beyond them and Canada.

In 1758, when George resigned from the army, he was an admired soldier throughout the American colonies. He returned to Mount Vernon, to be a Virginia planter.

4. *George Marries*

While George was still commander of the Virginia army, he met Martha Custis, a young widow with two small children. She was short, plump and lively with dark eyes and hair. And she was wealthy. When her husband died a year and a half before, he left her plenty of money, land and slaves. Soon after George met her they were engaged to marry. And on January 6, 1759 they were married.

Important people from throughout Virginia came to the wedding, including the British governor of Virginia, Francis Fauquier. George wore a blue suit lined with red silk, and his hair was powdered. Martha wore a white silk dress and had diamonds on her shoe buckles. They were married in one of Martha's Virginia homes, a home her family had named the "White House."

George was a good and loving stepfather to Martha's four-year-old son Jackie and two-year-old daughter Patsy. He gave them many gifts, including a new piano for Patsy. He spent the next sixteen years with Martha and her children at Mount Vernon.

George was forever busy there. He would rise early in the morning and have some tea and cake. Then he would mount his horse and ride out to check the work on his estate. He supervised the planting and harvesting of tobacco, corn and wheat and the fishing in the Potomac River. He owned more than 100 cows as well as horses, mules, oxen and chickens.

Like most other owners of large southern estates, George had many slaves to do the work. He was known to be a good master and wouldn't sell a slave who didn't want to leave. But still, his workers were slaves, men and women who were *owned* by their master and forced to work on his land or in his house.

George wasn't always working. He went to church. He enjoyed dancing. He rode on horseback to Alexandria to see ships launched. He played cards and gambled for small amounts of money. He especially liked to go fox hunting. He raised dogs for his fox hunts and he gave the dogs interesting names like Tipsey, Musick, Drunkard, Sweetlips and Rockwood.

George also served in the Virginia legislature. He was elected to the House of Burgesses in 1758. He was reelected again and again after that. George was generally quiet there. He seldom proposed any new bills or laws. But the peace in the colonies following the French and Indian War was coming to an end. And in the coming fight with the British, George would not be the least bit quiet.

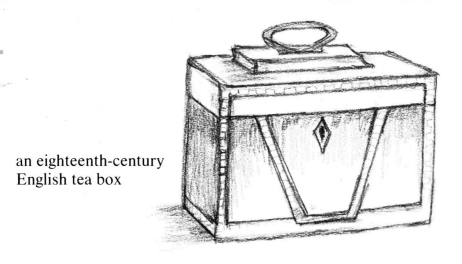

an eighteenth-century
English tea box

5. *Ready to Fight*

The British victory over the French in the French and Indian War was an expensive one. Britain was deeply in debt. The British people were already paying high taxes. King George III of Britain was determined to make the American colonists pay, too.

The American colonists resisted paying any of the taxes imposed on them. In 1773, to protest the tax on tea, colonists in Boston dressed as Indians and boarded a British ship. They dumped British tea into the harbor. King George was furious. New laws were passed in the British parliament. The Boston Harbor was closed. The colony of Massachusetts could no longer govern itself. Colonists had to feed and house British soldiers. The colonists called these new laws the *Intolerable Acts*.

In 1774 colonial leaders met in Philadelphia for the First Continental Congress. Following the leadership of George Washington and others, they voted not to buy British goods. A few months later, the colonies declared war on Britain.

The first shots were fired on the road between Lexington and Concord, Massachusetts. Shortly after that, George Washington attended the Second Continental Congress. He went dressed in the red and blue uniform he had worn during the French and Indian War. When others saw the uniform, they knew George Washington was ready to fight for American independence.

emblem on flag, 1775

6. *The Revolution*

There were many colonists ready to fight the British, but they needed a leader. At the Second Continental Congress, George Washington was named commander in chief of the American Continental army.

George Washington was modest. He told the Congress, "I do not think myself equal to the command." He was not seeking power, but he did accept the post of commander in chief because he felt he was needed.

George Washington did not hope to become rich serving his country. He refused to be paid a salary. He would keep an exact record of his expenses and only ask that they be repaid.

Being commander in chief was difficult. The soldiers were poorly paid. There was not always enough food or supplies for them. They were not well trained. Most of them didn't want to be soldiers. They only enlisted for a few months and then went back to their farms or shops. At times the soldiers didn't listen to the orders of their commander in chief. Sometimes even the officers refused to listen.

George Washington led his men to quick, surprising victories in Boston and Trenton. But the British, with their well-armed, better trained troops defeated George Washington's army in New York and Philadelphia.

George Washington and his army spent the winter of 1777–1778 in Valley Forge, Pennsylvania. It was a bitter, cold winter. Washington's men, many without shoes or blankets, suffered. But in the cold and the snow, the army was trained to fight. And in the spring good news reached George Washington. The French had signed a treaty with the new nation, the United States.

The French helped the United States win their war. In September 1781 in Yorktown, Virginia, George Washington led American and French troops against the British. At the same time, French war ships blocked the British from escaping across the Chesapeake Bay.

On October 19, 1781, eight days after the attack began, the British commander, Lord Cornwallis, surrendered. At the ceremony to mark the surrender, British soldiers put down their guns. Cornwallis laid down his sword. And during it all, the British band played a song called "The World Turned Upside Down."

It would be another two years before there would be peace and the last British soldier would leave the United States. But the war was mostly over after the Battle of Yorktown.

7. *President George Washington*

By November 1783 all British troops had left the United States. And early in December George Washington retired to Mount Vernon. He had not been a brilliant military leader, but he had used good, solid judgment. He was courageous and determined.

During the next few years, George Washington worked on the estate. And there were always plenty of visitors and many letters to answer.

George Washington was getting old. "I was now descending the hill I had been fifty-two years climbing," he wrote to a friend. He was still very strong. He could crack open hard-shelled nuts with his fingers and even bend a horseshoe with his bare hands. But he wasn't always healthy. At times he suffered from fevers, colds and various aches. His hearing and eyesight were poor. Most of his teeth had been pulled out. But George Washington would be called on again to serve the young nation.

In 1781, during the revolution, Articles of Confederation were written and agreed to by the thirteen states. The articles gave the central government of the United States very little power.

In 1786 there was a small revolt in Massachusetts. The state army stopped it, but it became clear to Washington and others that there was a need for a strong national army to defend the nation.

A meeting, the Constitutional Convention, was held in May 1787 in Philadelphia. George Washington was the leader of the Virginia delegation, People throughout the country knew he was a good leader and an honest man who did not seek power or money. They trusted him. The delegates elected him president of the Convention. A new constitution was written for the United States. It called for a congress with two houses, a supreme court and a president. George Washington was admired throughout the thirteen colonies for his leadership during the War of Independence. After the states ratified the constitution, he was elected the first president of the United States.

George Washington was inaugurated president in New York on April 30, 1789. People sat on rooftops to watch. They waved flags to celebrate.

At the inauguration George wore a brown suit, long white silk socks, a sword and silver buckles on his shoes. The newspapers of the day declared proudly that everything the new president wore was made in the United States.

People no longer knew what to call George Washington. Some called him "Mr. President." Others called George "His Excellency." And even others called him "His Majesty." People traveled many miles just to see George Washington. They wrote songs about him. They paid artists to paint his portrait. People loved George Washington because to them he was the symbol of their independence. They felt it was George Washington who held the country together.

George Washington was reelected in 1792. During his eight years as president, the capital was moved from New York to Philadelphia. And a new capital was planned along the Potomac River. It was later named Washington.

John Adams was George Washington's vice president. In his first cabinet were Thomas Jefferson, Alexander Hamilton, Henry Knox and Edmund Randolph. Jefferson and Hamilton often argued.

In 1793 several European countries were at war with France. Washington decided to keep the United States out of the war. A year later farmers in Pennsylvania refused to pay the tax on whiskey. They attacked those collecting the tax. President Washington sent troops to enforce the law.

President Washington signed a treaty with England which kept open the trade between the two countries. Spain controlled the Mississippi River. George Washington signed a treaty with Spain opening the river to American ships. He even signed a treaty with pirates in which the United States agreed to pay them to leave American ships alone.

George
Washington

Henry Knox

Thomas
Jefferson

Alexander
Hamilton

Edmund
Randolph

45

George Washington retired after his second term as president. He returned to Mount Vernon in March 1797. A year later he was back in Philadelphia to help raise a new army.

In December 1799 George became ill. Doctors were called. They poked him with needles and drained blood from him. It didn't help. Late on the night of December 14, he placed the fingers of one hand on the wrist of his other hand and counted his pulse. It was very weak. A short while later, at about ten o'clock, he died.

During much of his lifetime, George Washington refused to sell any of his slaves. In his will he left orders that the young slaves be taught to read and write. And he ordered that when Martha died, all their slaves be set free.

Throughout the United States, even across the Atlantic Ocean in Europe, people mourned the death of George Washington. Today we remember his life and honor him. So much is named for him—schools, bridges, streets, and towns. An entire state is named for him as well as the capital of the United States. His picture is on our money, on quarters and one-dollar bills, and on our postage stamps. On his birthday, February 22, a national holiday, we remember his great leadership during the Revolutionary War and his role as the first president of the United States.

Henry Lee, a former general and governor of Virginia, wrote how he and many Americans felt. He wrote that George Washington was "first in war, first in peace, and first in the hearts of his countrymen."

the U.S. Capitol in Washington, DC, 1988

INDEX

Text copyright © 1988 by David A. Adler
Illustrations copyright © 1988 by Jacqueline Garrick
All rights reserved
Printed in the United States of America
First Edition

Library of Congress Cataloging-in-Publication Data

Adler, David A.
George Washington, father of our country: a first biography/
by David A. Adler: illustrated by Jacqueline Garrick.—1st ed.
p. cm.
Includes index.
Summary: Presents a biography of the Commander in Chief
of the Continental Army and first President of the United State
ISBN 0-8234-0717-9
1. Washington, George, 1732–1799—Juvenile literature.
2. Presidents—United States—Biography—Juvenile literature.
3. Generals—United States—Biography—Juvenile literature.
4. United States. Army—Biography—Juvenile literature.
[1. Washington, George. 1732–1799. 2. Presidents.]
I. Garrick, Jacqueline, ill.   II. Title.
E312.66.A35 1988
973.4′1′0924—dc19   [B]   [92]   88-4691

ISBN 0-8234-0717-9

ℓ